The Goat's Gruff

THE URBAN EROTICA
FAIRY TALE COLLECTION

The Goat's Gruff

HONEY CUMMINGS

Dedication

To those early crushes that teach us not to let
love get away later in life!

Part 1

Sitting in front of his computer, Taylor Rolley stared at the GreetUp website. He heard rumors about those events with certain keywords, the ones with "naughty intentions," and wondered if they really existed. If he wanted to venture out and explore his unspoken sexual side (without judgment), this was the place to start. With a twist of his lips, he registered, then moved the cursor into the search box, first typing in "sex," followed by "intercourse." But no results popped up.

How do you find them? I have no idea which keywords to use!

His phone buzzed, his close friend Lou Brigadier texting him. He scowled at his phone. If it wasn't for Lou's wild stores stories about attending these sex parties, he wouldn't have found this site. Shaking his head, he unlocked it and text messages appeared.

[Lou: Did you register yet?]
[Taylor: Yes, why?]
[Lou: Sending you an invite to the party.]

In a flash, his phone and computer dinged in unison. There it was, the invitation from Lou titled, *Erotic Masquerade Party.* Taylor scoffed at the title.

Erotic... why didn't I think of that.

Scanning the details, he quickly realized they were very vague. A mask would be presented at arrival to keep all identities a secret before knocking on the door. *No names* and *no garments* were the only listed requirements.

The theme... *fairy tales.* Taylor rolled his eyes. *Invite only and come ready to swing.*

[Taylor: Isn't swinging for couples?]
[Lou: Na man. Just hungry peeps.]
[Taylor: I don't have a mask.]

[Lou: Just wear that art project you made in high school, dude. I'll pick you up at 9.]

Taylor swiveled his chair and stared at the homemade troll mask. It was meant for use in a play, but it creeped everyone out, so the entire production refused to use it, giving it to him as a consolation prize. The play had been called *The Three Billy Goats Gruff.*

The mask was solid white with warty features and tusks. It was designed so the lower half was missing, keeping the jaw uncovered so it wouldn't interfere with the actor's performance. He had only joined drama for that year, all for a chance to impress his crush, Celeste.

Fate intervened. We just weren't supposed to be together. Yea, I'm still salty even after all the time that's passed...

Taylor shook the memories from his mind. Instead, focusing his imagination at the present situation. He tried picturing himself naked, save for a mask, then shuddered at the possibility.

[Taylor: No one wants to fuck a troll.]

There was no reply.

Lou knew better than to respond to Taylor's excuse. If Lou ignored him now, it would ensure Taylor's attendance at the masquerade.

He sighed. *Nothing ventured, nothing gained*, he thought as he cursed silently into the bathroom, preparing for an evening completely in the nude.

Part 2

They arrived at the address, passing the security gate without trouble. Good thing since Taylor didn't want the guard to see how ridiculous he looked in a bathrobe and a handmade school mask. As they came around the bend, the house was huge. The only structure at the end of a cul-de-sac of empty multimillion-dollar lots. Still sitting in the car, Taylor watched as plenty of masked people in bathrobes entered the house.

At least I match the trendy crowd this time. Unlike high school...

Music pulsed through the air and the moonless night made him feel like he had been transported into an erotic version of the *Purge*. The question was whether he was the slayer or the slayed. Blowing a puff of air from his nose, he settled on becoming the latter. That's if he could even step out of the car and join the festivities. Shuffling in his seat, he tugged the robe's belt tighter as if afraid to reveal what lay underneath.

Shit, I don't think I can do this... this is a terrible idea. Curiosity killed the cat and will definitely kill me at this rate.

Knots twisted Taylor's stomach, making him sick as he looked at his own body, feeling betrayed.

I'm just an average guy without a six pack. At least I don't have a beer gut. Oh man, I can't... I don't have the body to pull this off.

Lou elbowed him, nudging his head toward a unicorn and fairy. They were naked, not a bathrobe in sight. The girls were curvy and beautiful enough to grace the cover or spread in a *Maxim*. Aroused, he remembered he did have one secret weapon.

At least I'm hung like a fucking horse.

He looked at Lou and they shrugged. At least there was eye candy at every turn. Inhaling deep, he gathered his nerves, regaining his lost confidence.

I can do this!

"Ok, so this is the place to be," Taylor declared. "But what do we do now?"

Lou turned off the ignition and twisted to face him. "Some rules. I can't have you fucking this up for me."

"Gee, thanks for the vote of confidence?" Taylor marveled. *Asshole.*

"Seriously, we can't use our names here. It's taboo and you'll get banned." Lou adjusted the polygonal wolf mask on his face. "The moment we step out of the car, my name is the Big Bad Wolf and you're Troll. Got it?"

"There's no way in hell I'm calling you that." Taylor tightened the cord on his own mask, thankful for how it conformed to his face. "Wolf. That's all you get from me, mutt."

"Fine, Troll."

Lou stepped out of the car, assuming his new identity despite how awkward he felt.

Taylor hadn't had a pretend name since online gaming back in grade school.

Troll followed as Wolf continued to lay the rules out. "Whatever you do, don't take off your mask, even if they insist. They'll ban you. If someone says no, leave them alone or they'll ban you. And lastly, don't dare imply you know the person underneath the mask or..."

"They'll ban you. I got it. Secrecy is top priority." Troll and Wolf went through the front door, entering the foyer. "So exactly how does... this... holy fuck."

What the hell am I looking at? So much... skin and moaning and... wow.

Troll's eyes scanned the grand living room. He couldn't tell what furniture filled the room, except the naked masked people filling the space. Masks came in different levels and colors; Furries, full-faced animals, masquerade, and even gimp masks covered the identity of the participants in the room. Blinking, he assessed each cluster as if selecting which porno he'd beat off to for the night. Sexual orientation had no restrictions as threesomes of all combinations groped each other.

So, this is what an orgy looks like in person.

One mask brought his eyes back to it with each attempt to take inventory of the events unfolding. It was nestled and half hidden behind the sea of bodies. Troll tilted his head, feeling nostalgic as he tried to get a clear view of a familiar mask. Two girls dressed as a bunny and fox were tag teaming at pleasuring a girl in an elaborate goat mask. Distraction took hold, his eyes falling to her lower jaw and exposed deep red lips. She bit them and he swore they locked eyes, a glint of surprise in her deep dark irises.

Does she recognize me? Do I know them?

His eyes lingered, travelling downward to her rosebud nipples and hourglass figure. Her skin had a healthy glow, even in the low lighting. As if alerted, Bunny and Fox looked his way, giving him a clearer view of Goat. Thighs open wide as fingers retracted from their play, the provocative view tantalizing on all levels. Troll could feel himself getting hard. He licked his lips; this was what he'd hope he would find. He refocused on the mask.

What kind of mask is that? It looks familiar.

"Wolf, how does this..." He turned to find his friend slipping away. "W-wait! What do I do? How does this work?"

"Fuck someone." Wolf waved him towards the room. "I think I found myself a Red Riding Hood to chase... enjoy!"

What does 'fuck someone' even mean?!

Wolf faded into a crowded hall of people drinking and groping. Looking back to the orgy in the room, he lost sight of the three girls that had tickled his fancy. On the far side, a centipede made up of a sexual chain was forming. On tables were fishbowls filled with colorful packages. He walked over to find a variety of condoms, even sample Viagra packs. He was crashing from sensory overload now that he lost his initial focus.

They don't mess around at these things. Granted, they did insist we come naked so... but what are the rules of engagement?

Two people brushed pass him, making him painfully aware he hadn't shed his stolen hotel-room bathrobe yet. He untied it and gripped the edges, his hardon glaring up at him like a dog begging for scraps. He should be naked like the others in the room.

Hung like a horse. Christ, it looks like I'm wielding a fucking broom handle. Then another harrowing thought struck him. *What if I smack someone with it?* He shuddered. *What the fuck have I gotten myself into?*

Closing his eyes, he let the robe fall to the ground among many others, even throwing his arms out like some kind of naked showman. He waited for...

What the hell am I doing? Everyone's naked and busy having sex, so why the hell would they be staring at me?

Snapping his eyes back open, he noticed the chain of sex had grown longer. His stomach knotted; the unrivaled exploration unfolding before him was too much. He scanned the room again, hoping to spot one of the three girls he had seen, but at last, no signs. Twisting around, he decided to explore the house. He'd never been in a mansion like this, so what did it matter if he took his time? Besides, he wanted to be more comfortable with being nude in the sea of cocks and pussies.

Looking at my competition, I'm in the younger selection as well as the bigger dicks lot. Maybe I'll get to let loose after all.

A smile came to his face. He was comparing himself with every man he passed, and it was enough to grow his confidence. On occasion, he would peek into the various bedrooms, watching what scenes were being played out. The women came in all colors and sizes. The Queen of Hearts was spanking an Alice, while she choked down the Mad Hatter's dick. He wondered if watching other couples while pleasuring themselves was taboo. His hardon was pure arousing agony as he enjoyed the roleplaying unfolding before him.

Wow, those porno parodies ain't got nothing on these people. He looks like a dead ringer for Johnny Depp.

Another room had Snow White being gang banged by all sort of forest animals, and he had to decline an invite as the horse pounding her waved him in.

Apparently, Prince Charming's horse wanted in on that action too.

The people, male and female, came in all shapes from plump and tall, to short and skinny. He'd never thought about what his physical preference would be until now. Granted, this place was the first time he could see the full menu up close and personal. His cock seemed to know, giving a clear sign of who he wanted to touch and those he didn't.

I like hips, subtle breasts, and lips that unfold like flower petals. Dark hair. Long, wavy but not curly... and down and falling over the shoulders. Not sure why, but dammit that's hot.

And between the thighs I like... I wonder, maybe try my luck with... dammit, I can't walk around dipping my dick in every vagina I find, can I?

He spotted a girl in a poodle mask and grew hard, his mind checking off his list of wants. She was only a little shorter than him, her hips large and curvy. She was as average as he was, but he liked that, and he wanted that. Unlike Wolf, it didn't take much to snuff out his self-esteem. Her hair was pulled back in a ponytail and she leaned on the wall, a glass of wine in hand. Puffing up, he approached her. He glanced down at his dick which stood at attention.

Here's goes nothing! Don't let me down, buddy!

"Hi there."

She turned, her eyes looking him up and down, lingering on his hardened length. "My, aren't we a big boy."

Score, now for the kill...

"I was wondering if..."

"No thanks. You're not my type." She shot him down fast and hard, his libido deflating some. "Besides, who'd want to fuck a troll."

The laughter from her stung. She pulled off the wall and walked away. Passing a table, she abandoned her wine glass and grabbed the painfully obvious older man in the horse mask. She gave Troll a glance, making sure he was watching. Groping the man's cock, she pulled his hand to her pussy, excited that he would watch her fuck another man.

Anger seeped in, and Troll turned away. *What a bitch. Well, I didn't want to fuck a gold digger anyhow. Dammit... I knew this mask was a shit idea. Wear that mask from high school, he said. It'll be fine, he said. You fucked me over, Wolf.*

He went upstairs, no longer pleased with the lack of action happening on the first floor. Peeking into the first room, he found Wolf. Indeed, he'd found a petite girl, in nothing but a red hood and plain white masquerade mask. She was on all fours atop a king-sized bed. The headboard banged against the wall and the mattress springs squeaked from their efforts. She panted, moaning with each thrust as her breasts swayed. Her skin was pale, hair blonde, petite—on all fronts, completely Wolf's type.

I swear. The girls he picks could almost pass as sisters. Like cookie cutter people. Blonde, nearly midget height, pale thin things every time. I want a woman that I don't have to wonder if she'll break under my touch like a porcelain doll.

Rolling his eyes, Troll continued down the hall. He didn't come here to watch his friend screw, but he needed to find someone to mingle with. *And quick.* Turning a corner, he froze. At the end of the hall he saw Bunny. The long white ears stood erect, covering her face like a superhero's mask. If Wolf had a gander at her, he'd want to hit that. Short blonde hair and a petite body, standing in the dimly lit hall.

Perfect Wolf bait.

Following her line of sight, a few more steps to clear his own view, he saw Fox.

Ok, two out of the three...

Her little top hat and ears complimented the orange and white whiskered animal face obscuring her face, enhancing her alluring black lipstick. She was taller than the majority in the hall, with athletic arms and a body fit for a kickboxer. Even her thighs and calves made it clear she either ran a lot or lifted weights heavier than what he'd ever attempt in this lifetime. Hooking up with a woman like that would make him feel like the porcelain doll.

That's two. Does that mean...

Sidling to the side, shouldering the wall of the hallway, he caught a glimpse of the third girl, the one he was after. Her pink nipples on tan skin, red lips like rose petals; he didn't need to see the mask to know it was her. He grew hard again and cursed under his breath. Shoving pass a fucking couple, he locked eyes with her once more. Brown pools looked on in shock as if frightened by Troll's approach. A smirk filled his face. For the first time in his life, he felt like a hunter chasing prey. His pulse raced as his heart beat against his chest. He leaned to the right, trying to catch a glimpse of her oh-so-familiar mask in full. Spiraling horns and a Y-shaped mouth gave it away at last.

She's the goat! That's what I'm after, I'm the troll. Dammit I want her so bad, I'm blue balling just thinking about what I could do to her. And why does her mask look so familiar? Where have I seen it before? The paint is amazing but...

A hand gripped his shoulder and spun him around. He closed his eyes tight. Goosebumps rolled across Troll's skin at the idea of someone seeking him out. His heart fluttered. This was it, his first invitation to fuck.

Please don't be a dude, please don't be a dude.

Troll opened his eyes and Wolf threw up his hands. "Whoa, watch where you're pointing that thing."

Glad his face was covered by the mask, Troll's cheeks heated with embarrassment and frustration. Looking over Wolf's shoulder, he snorted, seeing no sign of Red Riding Hood.

I don't have time for this...

"Don't tell me you two-pump-chumped her, Wolf."

"You're such a troll." He crossed his arms as if questioning how much Troll had seen. "Seeing your hardon tells me you still haven't fucked anyone. What the hell are you waiting for? Blue balls? There's plenty of naked people to pick from."

"Shut up." Troll rubbed the back of his neck, his groin aching for something palpable rather than simple eye candy. "I tried a few times, but no one is interested."

Wolf began to laugh. "Then don't ask permission. Show them the troll love they're missing!"

Troll looked over his shoulder, catching a glimpse of Goat's horns above the crowd of naked bodies. He swallowed, clenching his clammy fists. He didn't want to lose her again, but his confidence faltered as his eyes spotted Poodle. If that failed, what were the chances of him rebuilding his confidence in a matter of minutes? Recalling his past failed relationships, including the time he'd approached his longtime crush, it didn't seem likely.

Celeste shot me down. Granted, I didn't know she was dating someone at the time. Ugh, that was high school... She's long gone, and I'm at an orgy standing around with a monster-sized erection like a dumbass. Use it or lose it!

"Work them over how?" He turned back to Wolf, determined to change his fate. "We both know I suck in real life. How will a mask make a difference?"

"Dude, watch and learn." He shoved Troll to the side as he sashayed to Poodle.

"I tried to hit that, but..." his voice trailed off. Sucking on the side of his cheek, he discouraged himself from stopping Wolf. *I hope this fails. Or it will prove how pathetic I already feel.*

Wolf didn't hold back as he went in for the kill, first licking her collarbone, then carefully tracing the curve of her neck.

Troll cringed. *He can't be serious. No way in hell can this end well. Who fucking approaches a stranger, then licks them without a formal introduction?*

Circling behind her, Wolf slid his hand over her hip and ass cheeks before wandering back to face her. Troll waited for the inevitable face slap, but Wolf continued his attack, relentless and unapologetic. Pinching one erect nipple, then using his other hand to dive between her thighs. The bold move made Troll shift uncomfortably on his feet. Poodle abandoned her wine glass onto the floor, whimpering like a hungry dog as she arched into Wolf, giving him easier access to all the right places. This only made Wolf's hand dive deeper and he leaned down to suckle the other nipple.

What the fuck just happened? What the hell just happened?

Wolf looked his way before tossing his head back and howling into the ceiling. It was the most ridiculous thing Troll had ever witnessed in his life, or even in a cheesy porno.

Debbie Does Dallas made more sense than this!

With that, Poodle bent over, giving him a direct route. Wolf gripped her hips, sliding his cock right into her, hard and fast. She panted and barked with every thrust. The whole event grew wilder and more confusing to Troll as he took it all in, every detail.

I can't believe this. He shook his head. *What happened to the old man dressed as a horse? Did he even get this far?* Anger crept forward. *Goat's missing and now I'm watching this bullshit go down.*

"Poodles are such bitches," Troll muttered, stewing in his bitter thoughts.

Is he out of his mind? What made him think I could be bold enough to approach a naked stranger by sucking a titty or poking my fingers into their pussy?

Scanning the hall again, he locked eyes with Goat once more and grew hard again. Grunting, the sensation was agonizing now. Something about the way she moved, the jawline and hair cascading down her back in long dark waves. The divet down her back, the subtle rise and fall of her shoulder blades, even the dimples on her hips. Every part of her body appealed to him, one way or another.

God, she's gorgeous.

Looking back to Wolf, he had swapped roles, his dick already lodged in Poodle's throat. Wolf gave him a thumbs up before continuing his conquest. Troll cringed. His attraction for Poodle vanished as soon as Goat returned into view. It was then he realized his purpose; time to act out the role he had dressed for.

If everyone here wants to roleplay, then the Troll is after a goat. What was that tale? Oh yea, The Three Billy Goats Gruff. That's the whole reason why I even made this stupid thing for the Drama club. All I wanted was to get closer to Celeste, but they cancelled it and...

Cracking his knuckles, he charged down the hall. Wolf grabbed his arm, his cock still deep in Poodle's mouth. He pointed down and Troll scowled at him. He was making an offer and it sent a chill across his spine.

You can have that...

"Wanna piece?" Wolf grunted as he pulled out, taking a step back, enjoying his domination over her. "C'mon Troll, your part of my pack. Get in here."

Troll looked down at Poodle. On her hands and knees, she moaned and wiggled her ass as if to entice him. He could see the light catching her inner thighs; the woman was beyond wet and ready. Looking back at Wolf, he could see the stupid face his friend Wolf would make under it.

Two mutts deserve each other. Nothing sexy about her at this point.

"I got a goat to chase." A smirk crossed his face, the troll in him cackling.

The Poodle pulled herself off Wolf's cock, scoffing. "Did he just refuse to fuck me?"

"Yea. Apparently, you shouldn't have been a bitch to him earlier." Wolf gripped her ponytail and shoved his dick between her lips, silencing her. "No one fucks with the troll unless he wants to play with you first."

Part 3

It seemed like hours had passed. Troll had lost track of Wolf, even though the front window showed his car still parked under a streetlight. Snorting, Troll searched everywhere for the scrumptious goat. Waves of people had come and gone, new masks appearing to mingle in each new sexual delight. A fairy stopped him, groping his cock. A new constant manner of greeting in this surreal sexual world. Grunting, he scowled down at her, annoyed by the unwanted intrusion. By this point, he had accepted his inner troll and played the part with enthusiasm. It didn't take long before attendees expected him to be rude, harsh, and a bad boy.

Who knew talking down to people would invoke such priceless reactions!

She whispered promises as she stroked him, "I'll let you suck my sugarplums if I can play with your club, Troll. What say you?"

He laughed. *Okay, I give her credit on the pickup line, but I'm not in the mood.*

Leaning down, he growled. "A fairy will break under my mighty club. Besides, I'm hungry for goat and have no time to be gentle with the likes of you."

Her eyes widened and she knelt before him. "Please, oh please. Gobble me up, Troll! I am much sweeter than any goat. I am sure of it."

Begging... to have me. I don't even know what to do with this.

Troll's heart raced and he swallowed. She was pretty, light brown hair in a pixie cut. Her lips were thin pink lines on her angular face. The masquerade mask was colored like a monarch butterfly, and the wings she wore were a matching set. Shimmer paint and loose glitter decorated her body, making her look surreal in the chaos of the unfolding orgy. Her breath teased the tip of his cock, and it made his blood rush. She wasn't his usual type, but her bold approach had piqued his interest. And arousal.

I wonder... maybe I can just relieve this agony.

Curious, he leaned down and kissed her, deep and passionate, their tongues chasing each other in a dance. She suckled his tongue, refusing to let it go. He hardened in her grip. At last they broke away, her hand stroking his dick. The agonizing throb of his hardon returned to the stiffness he endured from the Goat's stolen glances. Grunting, he locked eyes with the woman under the mask, her mouth opening wide to take his length in.

Oh, sweet release is so close now.

He saw Wolf chasing another girl dressed as a fawn, antlers and full body paint. Following him to the hall, he saw *her*. Goat peeking at him from behind a wall, her eyes falling downward. The heat of the Fairy's breath against his cock startled him, forcing him to pull away. Her look of confusion made him smirk.

I can't. I don't want this. I want her more than a blowjob. Wait. Am I losing my mind?

"This isn't the taste you want. Fly free and seek out the Big Bad Wolf." He pointed in the direction Wolf had gone, in a dark hallway full of entangled bodies. "He's in the enchanted forest of moaning trees."

I sound so cheesy...

"Y-yes." She rushed off and down the hallway.

Well that worked a little too well.

Troll scratched his chest, smirking.

You're welcome Wolf.

Sighing, he peered around the living room, the designated *Orgy Centipede Room*. Nothing here enticed him, and he wished he was somewhere else, to join the hunt. But his chest ached. The Bunny or Fox were nowhere in sight, the Goat's closest companions. Perhaps he'd been chasing a lesbian trio, too tired of the party and they left.

No. I know I saw her, but she's gone again.

Troll reached for his back pocket and only managed to pat his bare ass, forgetting he wasn't wearing pants. He wondered, with all these people invited via a GreetUp post, maybe he could find her that way.

He searched the floor for his robe. *Fuck*, he thought, searching frantically for it. *Where is it?* At some point during the orgasmic activity, someone must've removed the robes. And it wasn't a short trip to the car. His anxiety crested as his eyes landed on the back door.

Surely a million-dollar home has a pool or garden of sorts. I need air.

He stepped into the night, chills crawling the entire length of his body. Cursing under his breath, he took in the pool area, barren and free of bare flesh. Inhaling deep, he calmed his nerves. A bridge cut across the center of the pool, and he smirked at the irony of it. As he walked across, he peered over the railing and frowned. The pool was void of water, the empty span reaching the concrete edge to the far right and left.

Infinity pool? Gotta cross the damn bridge just to reach the garden? Seems like a bad design.

Block this, and no one's crossing the bridge and going nowhere.

Leaning on the rail, he glared down at the empty basin. A grin came across his face. At last, the troll had his bridge. Though being naked in the cool night alone seemed pathetic. With no water, at least he didn't have to see his reflection. Nothing killed his self-esteem like catching a glimpse of his reflection, made worse by his troll mask and naked body.

Holy smokes. I just realized there are no mirrors here. Not one room, not any of the bathrooms, nowhere. Even if I wanted to see how ridiculous I looked, I'd have to return to my car and use the side mirror.

He reached under his mask and rubbed his eyes, freeing his mind from the oversaturated sex scene still raging inside. Instead, he redirected his thoughts on the starry sky, even the crickets chirping beyond the trees, where an owl hooted in the dark.

So, does that mean they drained the pool for this event? Christ, the water bill to drain it... no, to fill it back up. Is it worth having your home painted in bodily fluids? Then again, I suppose this keeps them from fucking in the pool until one of them drowns.

Part 4

"Trip, trap, trip, trap." The quaint female voice startled him.

He turned, and there stood Bunny. His heart raced. Once more, cute white bunny ears tilted with intrigue. She fit the role well, but she had ventured outside the safety of the mansion and dare cross his bridge alone.

They didn't leave. No. She didn't leave.

A smile crested his face. Unlike Goat, Bunny was short and petite. Her blonde wavy hair skimmed passed her shoulders, brushing against her small pink nipples. *Beautiful.* Sighing, he eased into his role as the troll of the bridge, luring the goat to cross the bridge into greener pastures.

"Who's that tripping over my bridge?" He cooed as he peered around, hoping to catch a glimpse of seeing Fox and Goat. But they were alone.

"Oh, it's only me," she replied, taking a few steps onto the bridge. "The tiniest one. I'm going to the garden to masturbate."

"Oh?" He puffed out his chest, stepping into the center to block her way. "Are you not afraid?"

She tilted her head, the white ears shifting accordingly. "Why? Should I be?"

"Doesn't it scare you that I may gobble you up?" Part of him felt silly for acting in this provocative manner, but he hadn't been the one to trigger the dialogue.

If this worked for the fairy, surely, it'll work now.

"Oh, no! Don't eat me." With her arms behind her back, she giggled. "Wait until the second one comes. She's much bigger."

He looked her over. If she passed, then surely the goat would come this way. Every time he had spotted one of the trio, the other two were close by. Scratching his chin, he wondered exactly how far he could play out the Three Billy Goats Gruff in this manner.

What the hell. Let's go all in.

"Fine." In high school, he had rehearsed the script a billion times since he'd been the understudy for the troll. Here, he'd have to improvise, to make the hunt exciting while he awaited his prize. "Be off with you, after you've kissed me."

Bunny let out a giggle as she skipped along the bridge, stopping at the peak with a big, toothy grin, devouring him with her eyes. He tilted his head, watching as she fingered herself, begging for him to lean closer. He obeyed and she kissed him, deep and passionate. Suckling his tongue while her fingers caressed his cock.

With each of her fingers, he moaned, hardening on command to her touch. *Damn, the rabbit knows how to kiss.*

Unlike the fairy, she was an expert at teasing his tongue with the tip of her own. He chased her, even within his own lips. Her fingers rolled over his swollen flesh, caressing under his shaft with just the right amount of pressure. Fingertips glided across all the right spots, her touch magical and silky. His breath caught as she circled the ridge of his cap. At last she broke free, ending their kiss and releasing his throbbing erection.

"Promise to gobble me up later, Troll."

Before he could come to his senses, she rushed off into the garden. He stared with wonder at how his night would end at this rate. He rubbed his cock, stoking it for a moment. The sensation of how she kissed him was far more tantalizing than the fairy before; he didn't want it to fade just yet. The numbing pleasure of his cock made his shoulders shudder.

To think a woman could have a touch like that.

"Trip, trap... trip, trap." This voice was sultry, pacing each step.

Troll spun back, and there stood Fox. His cock ached, excited at the prospect of seeing Goat. Fox had to be every bit as tall as himself, thick thighs and built like a female MMA fighter. He snorted, imagining how she could pop his head off if she maneuvered him in a headlock. She took a few steps forward and his heartbeat quickened.

I don't think I was well prepared to guard my bridge at this rate. Bunny nearly had me coming in her hand, I can't imagine how I'll defend against a girl this athletic.

"Trip. Trap?" Fox tilted her head.

"Who's tripping over my bridge?" He said in a questioning tone.

"Oh, it's me, Fox." She rubbed herself, her breast bulging out of her hand while the other dipped between her thighs. "I'm going to the garden to help Bunny play with herself. I'm rather in the mood to eat rabbit."

I'm starting to think I may want to eat Bunny too.

Troll's cock hardened further. If the three of them repeated their performance from when he first arrived, he hoped they'd let him watch and stroke to each of their movements. Who knew you could watch porn live? Fox came closer, so close that he could feel heat waving off her body against his torso and cock. She grinned, her painted black lips curving into mischief. The fox mask leered down on him, and he remembered it was his turn to respond.

"I'll gobble you up," he warned, nervous at how close her lips hovered to his.

"Promise?" she cooed.

Before he could reply, she kissed him. Unlike Bunny, she chased his tongue back into his mouth, their tongues rubbing together in a wrestling match. It wasn't the kiss he was reacting to this time. Her breasts pressed into him; nipples hard as she began to grab his ass. His hardened length slid between her soaked thighs, rubbing against her swollen pussy in the heat of her body. She was rougher than Bunny. Predatorial. He throbbed against her and she pulled away.

"Oh no!" She chuckled, making him chase her with his eyes as she crossed the bridge. "Don't take me. Wait a little bit and the Big

Billy Goat Gruff will come. She's the one you've been wanting to gobble up."

Laughing, Fox took off into the garden. At this stage, Troll turned to lean on the railing. His heart raced and chest ached, cock aching for more pleasure and more release. Skin against his skin, hot and silken, none of the encounters had been as sufficient as Goat's companions had been. Cravings rattled through him. Feral desire haunted him. He was so hungry now. This was the most foreplay and roleplay he had ever performed in his entire sex life. His nerves rattled him, his throbbing erection a reminder that everything he was experiencing was *real*.

No one will believe me that I trolled a bridge for sex. The high school play may have been cancelled, but shit, the encore performance is...

"Trip, trap, trip, trap." The female's familiar voice shook him.

It couldn't be!

Looking over, Goat had arrived. He froze. Her long wavy hair cascaded down her golden skin. She had ample breasts with rosebuds for nipples, her thighs as thick as Fox's own, but more of an hour-glass figure compared to her companions. Her exposed red lips bloomed like petals underneath the goat mask. Those brown eyes took his breath away before he realized the mask's detailing. The paint had obscured it until he could take a closer look.

The mask! I made that mask in high school!

"Trip, trap," she took a step closer with every word. "Trip, trap."

"I want to gobble you up." The words tumbled from his lips.

"I don't think that's the next line, Troll." She snickered, stopping in front of him, a hand placed on one hip. "Shouldn't you be asking who's tramping across your bridge?"

"I already know who's on my bridge." His heart raced with high school nostalgia building at his core.

I'd recognize that voice anywhere, but could it be... am I dreaming? I haven't seen her since graduation.

"In that case..." She came in, leaning close until her lips tickled his ear in a whisper. "Come along with your spear, poke me like you wanted that year, curl a finger around my stone, crush me under your body and bone."

"Then, I'll gobble you up, Celeste." He wrapped his arms around her, and she squealed. "I'll gobble up the goat, you're all mine! You stole my mask and I aim to take it back!"

"How'd you know it was me, Taylor?"

He began kissing and biting at her neck, his cock hard with excitement.

"My you're hungry!" She laughed, letting him take his fill.

He laughed into her. "Because I made each mask but I could never find the best of the goat ones to take home, so I settled for the troll instead."

He pulled away, Troll staring at Goat. Both smiled and in this imaginary fairy tale, they'd found what they'd missed out on long ago. Goat melted down to her knees. The heat of her hands sliding down his chest sent a shudder through him. Troll had his back against the bridge railing, unable to move. He grunted as the heat of her breath brushed against his throbbing erection. The tip of her tongue circled the head of his cock, making his blood boil. She kissed the tip, and he moaned. Lips hot against the tender flesh, she kissed and suckled on his hardened shaft, from base to tip, repeating the cycle.

How long have I imagined this moment, and never did I think it would unfold like this... wearing my masks!

Gripping the railing, Troll fought the urge to shove his dick inside her mouth. The way she worked his dick, gracing it with her lips before tickling the tip with her tongue, was mind blowing. He moaned, and she pulled away, leaving him cold. Grunting, he looked down. They locked eyes and she dropped her jaw open, her tongue stretching out like a red carpet. He reached down, a fist full of hair, and shoved himself between her lips at last. Slow, watching one another, he enjoyed letting her take him into the heat of her mouth. Any faster and he just might come too soon.

"I want you to gobble me up…" he muttered, shivering with excitement.

As he crested into the back of her throat, she moaned. Lips sealed tight around him and he throbbed in her wet warmth. She sucked, hard and long, drawing him deeper until the tip of his dick could go no further. Wiggling her head, he fought the urge to collapse forward. Every movement orgasmic and agonizing as she tried to hold back. She pulled and pushed, fast then slow. He fought his desire biting at his core.

Oh, if I knew back in high school that this moment would be waiting for me, maybe I wouldn't have been such a bitter asshole.

He hummed as her tongue wiggled and stroked the underbelly of his erection. Rocking his hips, he tilted his head back and closed his eyes. Each wave of pleasure made him tighten his grip on her hair. Her breasts rocked into his thighs, soft and hot against his skin, hardening her nipples. Biting his lip, he fought the urge to explode.

There's too much still to gobble up. I'm still hungry for more... not yet. Please not yet!

Looking down, he had swollen until she struggled to hold him in her mouth. He let go, pulling himself from her. She stood confused by the reckless abandon. He wanted to taste her as she had tasted him. Shoving her back, she stumbled into the opposite railing, the sharp cold metal making her gasp as he launched his attack. Troll suckled at her neck, working over Goat's collarbone until his hungry lips found his favorite spot. A moan escaped her, egging him on. He teased her nipple with his teeth, and she wailed with delight.

I want to hear her scream... I want to taste more of her...

Under him, he could feel her shudder with each taste of her breast. The jealousy of its companion striking him, he shifted to explore the other half of her chest. His erection hungry to have her yet still ignored by its master, the agony drowned out by the arousing sound of coos and hums. Denying his desire, he pleased her to no end, making her scream into the night air as he gobbled her down. Fingers knuckled on the back of his skull, encouraging him to suck her breast harder. A hot thigh glided up on his hip, signaling for him to travel deeper into the oblivion of her shaved pussy, already hot and soaking wet against his cock. Again, he refused to enter her.

I'm still hungry... I'm still tasting her body...

Abandoning his meal, he grew thirsty. A trail of kisses and lingering strokes of his tongue ventured across the valley of her stomach. The skin under his nibbles began rippling and quivering with want. He knelt slow and steady much like a setting sun as he sunk between her legs. He shoved the rising thigh over his shoulder, and she parted her red door, allowing him in. He licked her, hungry and needing. Now it was her turn to grip the railing, her body arching into him as she cried out once more. His tongue dove deep in her and her body shook. Never did he think her peach would taste so sweet, be so juicy with each lick and suckle.

This will be a night she'll never forget... I want her to remember me above all others.

The sounds coming from her were visceral, calling the attention of other animals from within the garden. Fox was the first to appear to feed on Goat's body. Hungry black-painted lips began suckling on a breast and before long Bunny had latched onto the other. Goat cried into the night, arching against the railing as Troll wrapped his lips around her clit. He teased the swollen jewel with the tip of his tongue. She shuddered, the leg on his shoulder shaking from the electric shock of erogenous pulses in every part of her being.

Oh, how I want to be inside her...

Two fingers slid into the wetness, hot and throbbing. A moan came from her trembling lips. Troll watched Goat's eyes roll back. Sucking and stroking, he demanded she not look away from his own glare beneath his mask.

She was breathless, breaking down from the exchange as she began to rock her hips, urging him to stroke deeper. Pulling out his fingers, he dove his tongue inside her once more and she cried in ecstasy, gushing with her orgasm.

I could drink her all night, but...

Glancing at the Rabbit then Fox, he could see how they played with themselves, thighs wet as they moaned into Goat's breasts adding to her own waves of desire.

Do they wish for me to gobble them down too? Or are they here to enjoy the festivities?

His aching dick only wanted one of them. Satisfied he had made her peak at last, he stood and raised her leg high on his shoulder, keeping her trapped between him and the railing. He waited, catching all three of their gazes waiting for the next act. Their stares flowed down to his cock as it rubbed on top of her pussy, keeping Goat guessing as to when he might enter her. Fox and Bunny bit their lips in jealousy.

All eyes on me... she's mine and only mine.

He slid slow into Goat, her tight, wet, heat making him tremble. Her breath caught as he dove deeper inside her still. Both his cock and her pussy were swollen and aching. Her wetness allowed him to glide inside her with ease. Flesh rubbing flesh as she tightened and arched. She moaned, unable to retrieve her shaking leg as he hugged it to him. His other hand gripped her hip, keeping her from escaping him. With careful timing, he moved in and out, slow and calculating as he felt her tighten.

I want to be deeper; I want to see her face clearly...

He let her leg down, pushing himself hard into her, gaining more depth. She panted, moaning with each stroke as they rocked into one another. Wrapping his arms around her, she responded by wrapping her legs around him. Fingernails clawed across his back as she clutched him, wild with passion. His skin pimpled with anticipation as he lifted her off the railing and aimed to escape. Much to Fox and Bunny's surprise, Troll walked away with Goat in his arms, cock still in her.

Dammit I want her to myself!

"Where are you taking me?" The heat of her breath against his neck made him throb inside her, and she tightened in echo. "When are you going to come?"

Soon enough, but for now this fairy tale isn't done...

"Come along with me my dear, if you please, I'll poke you all year, crown a finger with a stone, and crush your body with my bone." They laughed as they made it to the garden.

He laid her down gently on the hillside of soft, cool grass. Goosebumps waved over her skin as his body towered over her. He pulled off his mask, shedding his identity. Taylor thumbed her beautiful lips, his hand gliding up her jaw to remove the mask. Celeste laughed, rocking her hips as she began playing with herself, moaning. At last he had his wanton woman.

Her libido is uncanny. She might crush me, body and soul.

"You're so damn beautiful." He searched her eyes, the confession lifting a weight he had been carrying all these years. "I wanted to see your face before this all ended and, and…"

"Stop slowing down." She pulled him down, her breath like hot wax against his shoulder. "And fuck me hard, Taylor. Fuck me like I know you want, until I know nothing else but pleasure that…"

Taylor's arms dove under her, making her arch her back as another primal scream erupted from her. Taking a nipple into his mouth, sucking hard, he rocked his hips ever quicker. Oh, how tight she had become! She was hot and drenched, thighs slick. Their bodies yearning for more. Moaning, her legs widened to give him full access, her fingers gripping his ass. She wanted him to be deeper and he let go of her breast. Freeing his hold, he took both her legs over a shoulder. Leaning forward he pushed in her and she gasped.

That's the first time a girl took me all the way in… my god… to think this whole time…

He would slide nearly out of her pussy before returning, shoving himself harder and faster, earning gasps and shrieks of delight. Slapping against the bottom of her thighs, her fingers dug into the ground now, enjoying the angle he had forced her into. Taylor moaned, teetering on the edge of coming, losing his fight against his body. A visceral cry escaped her, head tilting back as another orgasm shook through her. His cock stiffened. Pulling out he started to cum, the hot liquid slapping against her abdomen. They looked to one another, panting and half laughing.

I can't believe I held out that long despite blue balling all night.

Celeste rolled up to her knees and started kissing him passionately. It was his turn to lay down in the grass. She straddled him, taking him inside her once more. He panicked. He was spent. She caught the glimpse of fear in his eyes and shushed him. A promiscuous look on her face as she caught her breath a moment.

"I want you to watch me play with myself while you rest."

Oh... my... I've opened Pandora's Box.

She rocked atop him, her breast swaying. She ran a finger across the cum on her body and they dove down to her pussy. Humming, her finger dove between them, rolling over her clit. Another hand smeared his cum across her body in the other direction before rising to grope a breast. The whole while he agonized over his throbbing cock in her pussy. Grunting, he thought back to the Viagra and cursed himself for not thinking to use some. She shifted forward, still grinding, still keeping him hard enough to please herself on. Her breasts pressed on his chest as she arched into him, peaking for a third time.

How many times is she going to come? And am I going to keep up with her?

"Oh, I could just keep coming again and again." She kissed him hard and wild. "You feel so damn good inside me, Taylor."

'Goat will crush the Troll, body and bone.' That's how that story ends. Is that how I'm going to end?

Snip. Snap. Snout.

A Bunny and Fox came out.

Panic waved over Taylor, the concept of pleasing all three terrifying at the rate things were going. Celeste sat up and began to place her mask back on. Taylor wondered where his had gone, still trapped under the crush of his life (in more than one way). Heart racing, he waited for what would unfold next.

Maybe I get banned… and I'll be okay. Right?

Bunny picked up the Troll mask. He had flung it out of reach during his declaration of love. Giving it to Celeste, Goat kissed him and placed it back on with delicate care. He wouldn't be banned tonight. This was a secret garden party, and he was the main course.

Oh no, I'm still playing the part of the troll…

"We need one more to join us, Goat," announced the Fox. "He can't keep up at this rate."

Phew, at least someone acknowledges that much!

Troll looked at the three animals before him, only one thing came to mind. "Go get the Big Bad Wolf."

Bunny and Fox looked at one another and grinned. "Big Bad Wolf?"

"Who?" Goat looked down at him, tilting her head. "You came with a friend?"

"Yea…" He cleared his throat. "Just let him know Troll sent you. He'll come running. Especially if Bunny asks him to."

Bunny giggled. "So, he's a sucker for blondes, hmm?"

"Oh no, he came?" Goat laughed, shaking her head. "Yea, Bunny, go find the Big Bad Wolf, but take Fox with you. She will ensure the chase will lead back into the garden."

Then they were gone.

At last, Goat dismounted and laid beside him, curling into his body as they stared up into the starry sky. He could feel the hum of his body relax, falling into a steady breathing rhythm, ready for another round. She nuzzled against his neck, her body tight against his side. It all seemed so surreal.

"Is this your first time?" Her voice startled him.

"At sex, no." He laughed, looking over at her. "At a masquerade sex party, yes."

She sat up. "To be honest, at first I wasn't sure it was you I spotted in the living room."

His face flushed, making him thankful the mask covered his face's betrayal.

"When we locked eyes, I couldn't see the mask. All I knew was I wanted a piece of you," he confessed.

"And how was it?" Her lips curled in a coy smile. "Hmm?"

Sitting up, he leaned into his knee, thinking. Her hair was a mess, leaves and grass sticking to their bodies. Under the dim light, their bodies glistened with sweat and glitter. He inhaled deeply, holding it then releasing it slow and steady.

He stared into her eyes. "You're more than I can handle," he admitted. "Like the troll in the story, the goat crushed my body, crushed my bone. It all belongs to you now."

"Oh, does it now?" She looked skyward, hiding her expression from him. "So, the troll has admitted defeat to the goat."

"Yup." Troll marveled over the cloudless night. "My body is yours."

"Prove it." She rose to her feet and stood before him.

"Prove it how?" Again, his heart raced as he sat there taking in her shapely body.

What the fuck did I just step in...

"Lean back," she commanded like a Pagan Goddess.

Swallowing, Troll leaned back, propping onto his elbows.

"Open your legs." Her gruff voice was hungry and full of desire.

He pulled his knees apart. *What the hell is about to happen to me?*

"Wider."

All the way, he exposed himself. His mouth ran dry as he felt helpless, his cock throbbing against his will. She dropped to all fours, crawling across the grass as she licked her lips. His blood rushed, his excitement growing. Grunting, his cock hardened, standing at attention for the Goat's hungry lips. Her loose wavy hair slid down his inner thighs, tickling him. He exhaled. A hot tongue licked slow and purposefully from base to tip. Lips cupped the cap and suckled. Moaning, he closed his eyes to savor the sensation.

She took him all the way in, the fleshy wall of her throat squeezing the tip. Some part of him wondered if she truly intended to eat him, to suck him dry. She bopped her head up and down his shaft, her drool trickling over his balls as she stroked them. She purred as she took him deep, repeating the motion. Abandoning the task, she crawled across his body. Lips as soft as rose petals kissed his hip, up into his abdomen. The tip of his throbbing erection rubbed her collarbone, between her breasts and over the swell of her stomach. Her tongue circled his own nipple before she suckled his neck. He didn't care she left marks across his body. He felt alive, on fire as she continued to ascend, his dick falling between her wet thighs, rubbing against her pussy.

My body is hers...

A rustle in the bushes made him jerk his eyes open, spoiling his ecstasy. Bunny burst through the hedges, a set of arms catching her around the waist. She squealed but was soon drowned out by a long howl. Wolf came into full view, nibbling at Bunny's neck, growling like an animal. It ended quickly as an athletic arm locked him into a head lock, pressing into one of Fox's breasts.

Yea, there's nothing sexy about that. His head may pop off...

"Holy smokes. Bend me over and fuck me." Wolf howled again, embracing his part full heartedly. "As long as Bunny can play too!"

Goat bit Troll's neck. "Ouch!"

"T-Troll?" Wolf escaped the headlock and looked on with surprise. "Found greener pastures, I see."

Goat started to kiss her way back down his body, making his dick throb. "You gotta help me."

"W-what?" Wolf tilted his head, taking count of the women. "Help you with them?"

Fox wrapped her arms around Lou, kissing at his shoulder and neck. "Yes, he said you would help us."

"They're hungry." Moaning, Troll tensed as Goat pulled his cock into her mouth once more. "I can barely keep up with her."

Bunny leaned onto Wolf, kissing him. It was the same move as before, and Troll knew he would be snared, lost in the rabbit hole. Bunny's talented fingers made Wolf hard in a single stroke, trapping him. Fox circled them, waiting for an opening. Wolf's hands slid down and gripped her ass, threatening to enter her. Bunny sunk to her knees and began suckling on Wolf's dick. Fox dropped on all fours and rolled across the grass, sliding between Bunny's legs. She began eating her out, making her squeal and choke down Wolf's cock even deeper.

"Oh, man. You hit the jackpot, Troll." Wolf hummed as he rocked his hips.

Troll moaned again, Goat's tongue slipping under his swollen shaft. She let go of Troll's cock and stood, his heart leaping into his throat. She paced around him, shooting glances at Wolf and Bunny. A part of Troll grew afraid. He hadn't imagined the prospect of sharing her with anyone else, causing him to sit up in alarm. But, Goat twisted her heel into his shoulder, slamming his back flat on the grass.

"I'm hungry." She laughed. "And you're invited to dinner, Troll. Like you, there's only one thing I want tonight."

In a practiced move, her knees were on either side of his face as fast as her lips were back on his throbbing cock. Her pussy on his lips, he wanted what she was serving. Moaning into each other, he licked and suckled as vigorous as she attempted. They rocked into each other, the pleasure rattling through them both. He knew he had hit a sweet spot as she faltered in her sucking. Tilting his hip, he repeated the flick of his tongue and suckled. Again, she faltered, pressing him to the back of her throat as she collapsed further on him.

She crawled away from him, but he gave chase. Troll gripped her hips, dragging her across the slick grass, and entered her. Her breath caught once more. He hadn't taken her yet in doggy style, and the way her body curved out and away added to his rising arousal. He slipped a thumb into her ass and arched and moaned, grinding into him. The way her pussy tightened around his cock told him she was more than willing to submit to his next desire.

"You ready for dessert?" He pulled out and pressed against her back door.

Looking over her shoulder, she licked her lips. "Make it a cream pie."

And this tale is told out.

Honey Cummings

A passionate, award-winning author of Fantasy, Honey has turned her aim toward erotica. Blending everyday scenarios, and crafting them into steamy, blood-boiling moments for every shade of audience. Whether you want something short and hot, like a student-teacher hook up to the more paranormal flair, where Sleep with Sasquatch has unexpected bonus, look forward to erotic short stories, novellas, and hopefully a Trilogy in the future. Honey's debut erotic short landed at No. 3 in Urban Erotica and continues to satisfy readers time and time again. Be sure to leave her a review and let her know what you think!

Follow Honey Cummings

amazon.com/Honey-Cummings/e/B07W-FX5FDX

AuthorHoneyCummings.com

instagram.com/authorhoneycummings

twitter.com/HoneyCummings2

facebook.com/Author-Honey-Cummings-101408818012749

MORE HONEY CUMMINGS BOOKS

Sleeping with Sasquatch
Cuddling with Chupacabra
Naked with New Jersey Devil
The Erotic Cryptid Collection

Laying with the Lady in Blue
Wanton Woman in White
Beating it with Bloody Mary
The Erotic Ghosts Collection

Beau and Professor Bestialora

The Goat's Gruff
Goldie and Her Three Beards
Pied Piper's Pipe
Princess Pea's Bed
Pinocchio and the Blow Up Doll
Jack's Beanstalk
Pulling Rapunzel's Hair
The Urban Erotica Fairy Tale Collection

Curses & Crushes: KU short story

Queen's Incubus: YONDER webnovel

WRITING AS VALERIE WILLIS

Cedric: The Demonic Knight

Romasanta: Father of Werewolves

The Oracle: Keeper of the Gaea's Gate

Artemis: Eye of Gaea

King Incubus: A New Reign

Queen Succubus: Holder of the Crown

Val's House of Musings: A Mixed Genre Short Story Collection

Writer's Bane: Research 101

Writer's Bane: Formatting

WRITING MM ROMANCE AS VC WILLIS

The Prince's Priest

The Priest's Assassin

The Assassin's Saint

The Champion's Lord: YONDER webnovel

Champion's Love: KU short story

More Erotica Books from 4 Horsemen Publications

ALI WHIPPE
Office Hours
Tutoring Center
Athletics
Extra Credit
Financial Aid
Bound for Release
Fetish Circuit
Now You See Me
Sexual Playground
Swingers
Discovered
XTC College Series
Collection

ARIA SKYLAR
Twisted Eros
Seducing Dionysus

CHASTITY VELDT
Molly in Milwaukee
Irene in Indianapolis
Lydia in Louisville
Natasha in Nashville
Alyssa in Atlanta
Betty in Birmingham
Carrie on Campus
Jackie in Jacksonville
A Humorous Erotica
Collection

DALIA LANCE
My Home on Whore
Island
Slumming It on Slut Street
Training of the Tramp
The Imperfect Perfection
Spring Break
72% Match
It Was Meant To Be... Or
Whatever

NICK SAVAGE
The Fairlane Incidents
The Fortunate Finn
Fairlane
The Fragile Finn Fairlane
The Complete Package

LGBT Erotica

DOMINIC N. ASHEN
Steel & Thunder
Storms & Sacrifice
Secrets & Spires
Arenas & Monsters
My Three Orc Dads: a Novella
Before the Storm: a Novella

ESKAY KABBA
Hidden Love
Not So Hidden
Signs of Affection
Deeply Devoted to Him
Honest Love
A Plane and Simple Connection

GRAYSON ACE
How I Got Here
First Year Out of the Closet
You're Only a Top?
You're Only a Bottom?
I Think I'm a Serial Swiper

Lookin in All the Wrong Places
What Makes Me a Whore?
A Breach in Confidentiality
Back Door Pass
My European Adventure
An Unexpected Affair
Finding True Love
The Dr. Cage Chronicles

LEO SPARX
Before Alexander
Claiming Alexander
Taming Alexander
Saving Alexander
The Fall of the House of Otter
The Case of Armando

ROBERT LEWIS
Someone to Love
Someone to Come Home To
Someone to Kiss

Discover more at
4HorsemenPublications.com

www.ingramcontent.com/pod-product-compliance
Lightning Source LLC
Chambersburg PA
CBHW020346110726
47898CB00003B/1059